Darkling

Darkling
Sheree Mack

Smokestack Books
School Farm
Nether Silton
Thirsk
North Yorkshire
YO7 2JZ

e-mail: info@smokestack-books.co.uk

www.smokestack-books.co.uk

Poems copyright
Sheree Mack, 2024,
all rights reserved.

ISBN 9781739473495

Smokestack Books
is represented by
Inpress Ltd

*Dedicated to all those people
who stood by me through
each and every shitstorm.
Thank you.*

Contents

Layer I
Cento for black birds pushing against glass	11
[frog-march]	12
The archives will never collect us in a good light	13
go seek help	17
How can a mother get over the decomposition of her baby's body in the back of a black cab?	18
how many more black women have to die in police custody?	19
Conjur Women	20
Why Bother?	23
Without the Gaze	24
back-in-the-day-memory as told by a black poet	25
white privileges.	26

Layer II
Run-of-the-Mill	29
found poem: hashtag black death	34
Don't sacrifice your skin for anybody	37

Layer III
how can we climb through the hold of the ship once more to come out moved?	43
we arrived here with stars in our hair and needles between our toes	45
stand on any corner of the fire city, look west to death	47
Resurrection	48
A true seal doesn't need to be told her worth, she wears the crown	49

Layer IV
akin to a child-like wonder   53
dark morels nestle under my left breast, wide and soft   54
Morchella Elata – Black Morels   56
women within the earth will welcome me once more   57
'When a woman pushes a person out of her pussy
it transforms her'   58
i kinda wanna crack horology wide open   59

Layer V
Llyn Manod, Gwynedd   63
Praise to the Lupine   64
Listen   65
Learning to Breathe with/in Nature   66
The first crisp days of autumn give them to me   67
Druridge Bay, Northumberland, 2021   68
we only protect what we love   69
i am becoming my mother   71

Layer VI
Playing Palimpsest   75

Layer VII
healings   91
womb is the ancestors   92
aftersong   93
Surrender into Blackness   94

Notes   96
Acknowledgements   100
Works Cited   101

Cento for black birds pushing against glass

The first breath comes from early morning blossom.
Rain falls short. Look. The unbuckling sky. Rain.
There's an old pain. The memory of water keeps
flowing heavy with blood. Bloodhounds catch the scent.
Black bodies packed into boats & the tide still rolling in.
A corpse dangling from the end of a rope. Justice they say.
& they cut off parts for souvenirs. Within these city walls
there is no room for self-love. Grin, keeping grinning
at the camera. My heart catches on fire as it could easily be my story.
My body. Along blood lines, pumped into the centre of the wound,
it's the body that remembers as tonight this river will receive
a burden like black morels crushed under foot.
Pull the earth on top of her, turn her black face away from
the light. I cannot. But they've got the centuries' old tradition
to fall back on; the rich white man & the Black woman
kept close in the big house always ready to be cracked open.

[frog-march]

face down between four
coppers each holding a limb
bête noire
black body breast belly
beached [beast] down

the veil of deception
traced with domination
bears heavy on broken wings
wings never meant to fly

ruddy red blood runs out
the black [beast] awakens
thrashes and writhes
bucking bending backwards in time

surrender my beauty
belle divine
there's only so much
a human [beast] can spine

The archives will never collect us in a good light

1.
In the far-reaching twisted media archives,
they've glassed us up & our blackness in.
Our blackness is wholeness,
the whirling & worrying on water.

Our bodies light up the world,
our fighting flesh. & yet here,
we're subdued to meat,
our humungous hearts trophies.

Every whiteman has stood on our backs.
Every child has suckled on our breasts.
Mighty arms which wrapped everyone together
are led to extinction in this humid hold.

In the dark, our magnitude is masked,
our monumental strengths redacted & erased.

2.
In pursuance of the powers vested in me by section 32 of the Police Act 1964, I, Right Honourable William Whitelaw, one of Her Majesty's Principal Secretaries of State, hereby appoint the Right Honourable Lord Scarman to inquire urgently into the serious disorder in Brixton on 10 to 12 April 1981 and to report, with the power to make recommendations.

Stories keep being told; this is a tolerant country.
It's official. Britain is tolerant, fair & just.

There isn't a race problem. Never was. Never has been.
People who are different are treated the same.   ,

Tolerated. As long as we don't make a difference.
Small 'minorities' are accepted as long as we stay small.

Get to 'swamping' & then we become a threat.
We start to threaten the whole fabric of British superiority.

Tolerance, liberty & civic duty, such values go out
the window, when the nation's anxieties are raised.

Fear. & the country's doors are closed.
The drawbridge raised.

Their bulletproof shields driving us back.

3. History Repeating Itself
Black trauma is never given space to heal because we have to make sure the white people who hurt us don't feel too bad about it. Even as victims, we're told to care about the feelings of those who harm us.

the sky feeds us continuous greys & harsh words from ugly white mouths,
& yet we enter the frame

clasped hands in lap or right hand on chest, like in allegiance, chin forced
upwards as best clothes stiffen backs & resolve

a practiced pose, easy to send back home as proof of promises made good,
mother country come good, it's expected

the camera will point & lie for generations; the flash will blind us,
to our naivety, to their ungratefulness & their hate

4.
Atlantic Road, tight with heat,
round the rubble, the dying screams,
& pigeons, we wander.
A boy's t-shirt clings to his back.
A woman's shopping rumbles
over the cobbles & we,
the Black community, ready.

Your anniversary of our arrival
& you say not to bother.
Not to bother making a song & dance.
No heart felt effort here.
We push out, go back to the beginning
& wonder when our dreams of making
it good & sweet as honey died.

We roll with the flames, fear
bounces over the edges & we seize
our freedom: the spaces we've been denied.
Smelling of nutmeg & winter, any warmth
is just out of reach in our cramped rooms.
We take comfort in each other, rallying
ourselves before another layer of flesh
is skinned as we push against
this harsh, white-washed world.

5. we were born under a beautiful harvest moon
*The evidence is a tumultuous, violent crowd determined to execute
and executing a common purpose to attack the police with
alarming and very dangerous missiles is too plain to be challenged.*

we dance with the flames

our bodies slathered in light

years to come, we'll be seen

in slow motion, again & again

arms raised, bricks in mid-air thrown

reaching for what was promised.

we are the sea – tides juicy with man'o wars

funny how much authority desire has over us

we want to be on the inside, wear the crown

instead, we're always drowning in the shallows

trying to make something out of nothing

make tenderness towards the backs turned.

go seek help

for Renisha McBride

It's night, there's a porch
and a swing set. It's still.

A teenager's lying on her back
at the bottom of the front steps.

Arms splayed above her head,
legs stretched out straight.

Pieces of bloodied hair,
brain and flesh are splattered,

matted down her white blouse.
Her face is gone,

blasted away by a shotgun
through a screen door.

A white man
fears for his property.

Her hands are empty
yellow palms open to night's skin.

How can a mother get over the decomposition of her baby's body in the back of a black cab?

for Sarah Reed

I wish I could hide you behind my red dress,
still holding you close, my lilac.

How your skin whitens in this cramped air.
You're lost to me, as I'm lost to me.

Will we find each other again? Inside,
I have silenced my screams to a wound

bleeding into your blanket of white-
hate-bandaged around you, my baby.

Who called the Hackney cab?
Who opened the door?

Open your eyes, my love, haunt me
with your cries, anything but this, this stillness

this whiteness. Thirty minutes too long
I held you from the hospice

to the undertakers. The smell of vomit
in the back seat. Did that come from me?

You're a dead weight, you're no longer
mine. I carried you for the same amount

of time you lived. Let me take you inside
once more. I will breathe for two once more.

how many more black women must die in police custody?

after Kali Nicole Gross

behind steel bars
upon concrete walls
smeared with shit & blood
a shadow swings

bed sheets
like gnarled roots
exposed

twisted around
a creaking branch
upholds old customs

justice unbalanced
by race

if she was white
she'd still be alive

.fact.

.dead.

she failed
to signal
a lane
change

Conjur Women

after Romare Bearden

'*Above all else, our politics sprang from the shared belief that Black women are inherently valuable, that our liberation is a necessity.*'
The Combahee River Collective

1.
Rain. Drizzle. That fine kind that can soaks right through. My raincloak – turquoise, from Iceland, the island – with a big enough hood to protect my hair.

Walking through the hustle of urban life, blossom stains the pavement like little pink moons.

I see her walking towards me. Another Blackwoman. As we walk past each other, we smile. In that split second,

our gaze says,
I see you; I value you; you are recognised.

We walk on through the rain, sparkling.

2.
You've got to respect racism. From centuries they've manufactured lies. Backed up with scientific 'evidence' and disseminated to justify the superiority of whiteness, it is truly remarkable. A great feat of ingenuity. I wonder, within a few more centuries down the line, if whiteness will still reign supreme or if with a loud bang everything will plunge into darkness?

3.
The message read:
Apologies for the short notice
but this has been planned in a
deliberately spontaneous way.
This is a Black Feminist intervention
within the white cube.

We come to reclaim space.
We come to recover our rituals.
We come together as a collective.
Women only (children are welcome).

4.
Daily,
I walk into the sea.
Under her spell,
I release my pains,
& all identities.
Soothed
within her chilly embrace,
all ugliness thrown upon me
washes away.
It only takes a moment to escape,
to take flight through the waves.
To remember.
Afterwards, I can re-enter
the circus & continue
to pull magic
out of my arse.

5.
I stand here as a Black Feminist invited to talk about our activism as cultural work, how the personal is always political and the political always personal. What does it say about this conference when the only Black faces, I see are the ones next to me on this panel? Our stories blistering on our lips, we're ready to testify about our pains and our sufferings. But we're sick and tired of always having to go back to basics, as if you never listen, like you never learn. Why do we have to educate you about us, when from first sight we've had to learn about all your shit? How you like your tea, why you need to keep the light on at night and how to make you feel loved. We're always searching for the right words to make you listen, as our words are forever falling to the bottom of the ocean. Words forever being lost in your handbag of white privilege which you fail to check at the door, again and again.

6.
Oozing wounds, daily. Festering.
The tip of my tongue, my throat, my windpipe
thwarted.

Sometimes, my wounds twist like a tempest
through my ribcage, aching deep inside. Hidden.

Nourishing, healing vibes need to be fed along my blood
lines, pumped into the heart of my wounds
as it's the body that remembers.

7.
Dialogue is good.
But we're hardly going to get anywhere
if you insist on casting me as the monster.

Why Bother?

A beast is always going to be a beast, right?

Sing – bird – sing. Open your throat wide & sing.
Who cares if you're all alone in your beauty?
– Sing.

Trying to fit my foot into someone else's boot
distorts my whole body, my whole being, never mind my foot.

Pat – pit – Pat – pit. The rain falls.
The rain continues to fall on every shade of green.
Such a pleasant land indeed.

Indeed, I want to be purple. Maybe
sometimes shocking pink.

Without the Gaze

domed droplets cold on blades
blossom blown bushes taste bruised
flap flap glide glide flap flap
padding paws – away black dog away
thin mist aniseeds my skin
cup a handful of the fallen
& smell purple

back-in-the-day-memory as told by a black poet

The orchard is a rare find.
I never thought of the blossom.
The pure smell lingers down the road,
undulating. From the back,
she squeals for the hidden dips,
felt within the core. Always afterwards.

His neck is red. Pains in his head.
That must be why he seldom smiles.
I know I put them on a pedestal.
Yet, I still want what they had.
How they kept the passion from melting.

The alternative is now 'Other'.
She invites me as things get political.
It reminds me of those actresses
who accessorise at the awards
with women of colour.

Perhaps, the sea is history
and with cobbled streets along the docks,
I thought we were going somewhere.
Same images played over and over again,
the trickster used my face. My skin. My voice.

I say, give me green fields and bleating sheep,
for I can see behind their stares.
Some days, I smile them away. Other times,
I visualise punching their eyes out
then laughing into the holes of darkness.

white privileges

upon a turquoise threshold
I hold on to you tighter
sensing shifts

I stroke these moments
of damaged velvet with
desperate need

hearing you breathe
no longer I & you
no longer black & white

I wish I could see
with your eyes
walk with your privileges

I swallow my words
like glass become tangled
in sheets of doubts

at the closed door
wondering the direction
the sun's rays will fall

I want the feeling of light
I want to be turned
on that pedestal

Run-of-the-Mill

In response to The Enchanted Mill, Franz Marc, 1913

1. The Submission
The light holds such promise.
Earth sprouts blocks of green
trees. Cubes of water curve as angular
animals drink beneath the red wheel.

Sun-kissed playgrounds hold Black
kids, with afros and hijabs.
Mouths wide sprouting chants,
'Black Lives Matter!' under red clouds.

Birds flock, splash into the flow,
boom boom boom, flash of grenades.
Their tunes ripple within the flow,
drumming rubber bullets off flesh.

A harmony of colours and cries,
a moment ripping through history,
where white people protest at the loss
of property rather than Black lives.

2. The reply to the submission
Many thanks for your poem, which I would like to publish. I've scheduled it for 30 June, at 9.00am. But would you be willing to lose the 'white' in 'where white people protest at the loss/of property rather than black people.' just leaving it as 'people'. Because it is a bit of a generalization (I think the majority of people, myself included, and most of my readers/contributors would not think this way), which some might find offensive?

3. The response to the reply to the submission

Thank you for accepting my poem.

(My strict West Indian
Dad brought me up to have manners.)

In answer to your request, to omit the word 'white' because it might cause offence, to yourself and your readers, is no.

(I didn't beat around the bush,
as that could be taken as being
impolite, no? And what I wanted
to ask was, 'Would you be willing
to lose "white"? Go through life
as a Blackwoman? See the world through
my eyes? And while we're talking about
willingness, would you be willing to place
"white" in front of your use of the term
"people" so we're all on an equal
footing?' But that would definitely be
impolite. Right?)

To you it might appear as a generalisation, but to my story and truth, the majority of people who are complaining about damage to property due to the USA protests, not riots, are white.

(Page title: 'Anger in the streets'
Headline: 'BUILDINGS MATTER, TOO'
Byline: 'Yes, they can be rebuilt,
while lives are lost forever.
But that doesn't mean they will be.'
The Philadelphia Inquirer, 02/06/2020}
FUCK, another bad editorial decision.
And if we're going to be talking about
generalizations: Black people are good at
basketball. Black men are criminals.
Blackwomen are angry.)

And it is being proven again and again that the majority of people causing the damage are white.

(Some looters, meanwhile, aren't
affiliated with protesters' causes
at all. Instead, they seize the moment
to cause chaos and destruction.
This might be what's happening in videos
where white people can be seen knocking
out windows and ransacking businesses.
{*The Atlantic*, 02/06/2020} **)

** I've gone to the trouble of providing the evidence for you now, citing the sources too, all academic like because I want you to have all the facts. But I felt in my core that there was no use in grabbing the evidence to show this [white] bitch because it wouldn't have made any difference.***

*** Does my use of [white] bitch offend you? But come on, if you saw me, and I rubbed you up the wrong way, wouldn't you call me a [Black] bitch?

But the important point here is that property is valued more than a Black person's life.

(Growing up we weren't allowed to watch
Roots, the TV series created from the Alex
Haley book. But one time, while away from
home visiting Nana and Granddad, it was on
the TV. The adults were chatting forgetting,
me and my sister were there. We watched as
Kunte Kinte got his foot chopped off because
he just kept on running. Of course, to my young mind, this scared me. Not because I identified with the Black man. No. Because I liked to run.

That is the important point here, is it not? For me anyway.
To omit the word 'white' takes away the whole premise of the piece and offends me.
(Maybe I do write to offend. Maybe I want to
Rile you into a reaction. Or maybe I want to
write the words and stories that I never read
growing up. Maybe I want to write my body
into existence, to the point that somebody else
reads my words and is compelled to stands
with me, fights for my wellbeing. Fights to
make sure I'm recognised as having value as
a human being.)

In this climate of change and discussion, if you didn't see or feel this, then I suggest a book you might be willing to read called White Fragility, Robin DiAngelo.
(I suggested this at the time, as a way of
getting in the term 'white fragility'. You
know that way you, Dear white reader,
get defensive when you're challenged
about your ideas surrounding race and
racism. And heaven help us if you feel
implicated in white supremacy at all. I
know from experience, a message coming
from my mouth is much better received
when coming from the mouth of another
white woman. Something about listening
and identifying with the speaker. But
since recommending this book, I've heard
issues about it perpetuating its own kind of
racial prejudice.****)

I withdraw my poem from your publication.

(And really, I felt like a fool. Or like someone who'd forgotten their place. I thought we had a connection. You've loved my other work, which was dripping in Blackness. What's the different this time?)

****Sorry if *White Fragility* was in your reading list. If I had a do over with the email, I'd suggest *Wretched of the Earth* by Franz Fanon, critiques colonial violence and inspires the revolution.

(There wasn't even a 'please.')

found poem: hashtag black death

after Sharon Hurley Hall

is on trend

black people trend
when black people die
you have a black body
& it shows up in all
your feeds   trending
images being shared

hashtag black death
hashtag black body
hashtag black trauma

black people are not trending
when we are calling out
white supremacy

black people are not trending
when we are calling out
discrimination in the system

black people are not trending
when we are calling out
injustices of racism, sexism, ableism,
hetrofuckingnormalcy

black peoples are only trending
when black people are dying
when black people are killed
for walking, running, driving,
dancing, breathing

black people trend
when black bodies are terrorised,
brutalised & dehumanised
black bodies trend

our trauma is a trend,
the black body as an object
is a trend

when black people try
to explain our situation,
explain the trauma,
try to explain, display,
plead how black lives matter,
then we do not tend,

black people are not a trend,
black people's voices are hidden
by the algorithms,
black people are invisible, silenced,
shamed, disregarded, cancelled.

black people do not trend
when we make ourselves the subject,
when we take our agency back,
when we take our power back
when we take our stories back.

black people do not trend
when black people speak up
about touching our hair,
for the fetishisation of our bodies
for the raping, pillaging
& extraction of our souls

hashtag black death
is on trend

black people trend
when black people die.

Don't sacrifice your skin for anyone

1.
driving on the open road
a wide blue sky beckons me on
tarmac whistling
from mounds of snow sun-bleached grass waves
I'm heading in no particular direction
stopping when the mood takes me
eating fish, talking to the locals
burrowing my toes in black sand
soaking up this slow, old-fashioned breath of life

2.
You have to respect ice. It holds ancient air. Air bubbles from centuries past that can be drilled out and analysed. Retrieve vital information about climates past. Like the rings within trees, each bubble holds clues about life. I wonder if they drilled through me, pulled out bubbles of air, what secrets they'd find?
I say good luck to them. I live in this body and I still don't have a clue about who I am from one moment to the next. The key to that knowledge is ancient.

3.
I'm late collecting my luggage. I'm one of the last few to go through security. A uniformed man and woman stop me. Ask me to follow them to an inspection area. No one else from my flight is there. While the woman switches on their x-ray machine thingy, the man seizes my luggage. He asks me questions at the same time.
Is this your first time in Iceland?
Where are you from?
How long are you here for?
Why are you here?
Are you here for work?

From the stopping and searching and questioning, I can't help but answer the questions with attitude. Short and snappy. There's tension in my voice that comes out sounding like impatience and disbelief and exasperation.
All the time they send my luggage through the conveyor-belt sensor backwards and forwards, pointing things out on the screen and saying things in Icelandic to each other. Then they put on the blue rubber gloves and start to open my baggage. Pulling things out, moving things around.
The woman pulls out my coffee and my squeezy lemon and bottle of honey. And holds each one up to the man. I verify what they are. Then, I'm free to go.
Have a nice stay now. Enjoy your visit. Smile smile smile.

4.
I sleep in the cradle of mountains. The silence is soft and muffled and heavy. It rains overnight. Looking out across the fjord I see black, brown and sage as the landscape loses it white mantel. Life is coming back to the Western valley. An icy wind still blowing in from the Arctic, but the land is on the turn and it reflects in my mood. I find myself humming as I fix coffee. My hips sway between the cooker and sink in the cabin. My cheeks are flushed and even without looking I know my eyes are sparkling, matching the ice crystals in the remaining snow.

5.
In the 9th century, the first Viking to discover Iceland was Gardar Svavarsson. Through harsh weather, while sailing from Norway to the Faroes Islands, Gardar's ship ran off course and ended up at a strange, new island. His reports of the island must have been good, because Norsemen and Celts followed him to Iceland and settled. With little to no significant immigration since this period, Iceland remains genetically homogeneous. Isolated. Nordic. White.

6.
The smooth fold of the map between my fingers brings me right back into the excitement swelling in my stomach. I'm actually doing this alone. Driving the ring road around the island, with only Beyoncé to keep me company. *Lemonade*. Empowering. The glacier lagoon is just there by the side of the road. It's weird how close it is to modern civilisation. I soak it all in. This luminous turquoise bluey-green river with floating icebergs. Bulky icebergs that are melting. Rapidly. Tourists take photographs of themselves with a foot propped up on an iceberg like hunters displaying their kill. I feel disgusted. But how am I any different? I came on a whim; I came on a credit card.

7.
Foreigners in Iceland are required to always carry a passport or some kind of legal identification. The law also states that the police can search your home if they suspect that you might be attempting to defy their immigration laws.
It's human nature to clump ourselves together into groups of people that look, talk and think the same. It's about feeling safe. Throw someone different into the mix, people get uneasy and the seeds of prejudice bloom.

8.
Coppery red flat tops
curl in towards
soft shiny centres

The symbiosis of a fungus and a green alga, lichen is the first plant to colonise a hardened lava field. Versatile and hardy, it thrives to survive under harsh, volatile conditions. I marvel at its tenacity, wishing I was as robust. Clinging to rocks, tree trunks and wire, lichen grows and glows. Branching and shrubby, once upon a time I would have been too afraid to look so closely, to distinguish life amongst the dark holes of decay. Now I don't look away. Now I see the beauty.

9.
During the interwar period, there was a nation-wide building of swimming pools. Being able to swim was very important for a country heavily reliant on fishing. It was a matter of safety. Each village has a swimming pool. It's a place of worship with sauna and coffee and community.

10.
Inside a bookshop in Reykjavik, on the top floor, is a coffee shop. I order a latte and search for a seat. A man looks to be leaving. I utter the word, '*Excuse…*' when he looks at me and shouts, '*Get the fuck out of here, you fucking nigger!*' Followed by a guttural laugh in my face. I stand with my mouth open. Speechless. I close my mouth and walk away.
I feel as if I've been slapped in the face. I feel exposed. I sit in a corner. My vision blurs. I feel a wetness in my hands. This man's guttural sounds continue. I realise he must be mentally unstable. There has to be something wrong with him. In that moment, I'm glad I didn't respond to his abuse with abuse. It's not part of my make up. I know that much.

11.
You have to get naked into the showers first before you put on a swimming costume. Wash all your parts especially your armpits, genitals and feet. Then you're allowed into the pool. I hesitate before I haul my Black body in there. I fear there'll be security guards overseeing the washing of the bodily parts.
The pool is busy. I get in. Water not too hot and not too cold. Just right. I just swim for the hell of it. Allowing the water to slide off my shoulders as I extend my arms in breaststroke. Allowing the water to glide between my legs as I repeat the action like a frog. Stretching my body out and then contracting. Expand and contract. Expand and contract. I feel energised and free and comfortable. I have a feeling of gratitude towards my body. I feel calm and centred and present.

LAYER III

how can we climb through the hold of the ship once more to come out moved?

after Saidiya Hartman's A Venus in Two Acts

moving through strait, a liquid place, caked with sea-salt
   & sharks,
a harshness coats our throats as bodies touch,
                                       flesh upon stolen flesh

we will be reduced to a slip of ink in a captain's log, *dead girl,*
silenced within an archive built on a foundation of
   violence.

we, shackled to each other's story, sharing the same heart
                                 held between us like home

two girls died on board the *Recovery*. & Venus was her name.

in this watery world-less ship, liquid black ghosts conjured
   up,
their vibrating voices, surface through the grains,

like blood seeping from the bodies whipped to ribbons,
shreds of life haunts
                                our dreams of walking
                                across the ocean floor
                             or flying into the darkling sky.
                                        FREE.

our memories banished from the ledger, *how can the scenes of our subjection be explored without the violence entwined?*

how can we be reclaimed without the story always ending with our death?

we litter this floating world like waste.
no. let's be poetic, like confetti,
bloated by death & sea.

    numb, blown away, lost to the waves, harsh hands & history,
        we wish only to be remembered fully,
            not minor characters
            but centred, seen,
   rounded in the hull, in wild ambition, *in the wake*.

found poem: we arrived here with stars in our hair and needles between our toes

after drea brown

be autumn/ be siskin/ be slick
twilight licks our dark skin

deep within the forest
straining through spruce/ larch and pine

(trial & error I learnt their names/ names
are never easy on black bodies)

living within the unknown (out)side
where history is wet/ with memory/ & muchness

within the shadows/ within the wake
we search/ for a tenderness in the brokenness

breathing in/ in-between spaces
tongue locked/ tongue packed/ tongue tied
we be/ but not be/

unfurling like tight fisted ferns
brown bruised/ violence against ourselves

into the woods/ in flight/ in creep creek/
in restless/ motherless moan

shapeshifting/ combing the black air/
what would happen/ if we linger

in the midst/

/////////slow/////////down/////////slow//////motion////////

refusing to be absent for
ourselves/////////slow///////breathing//////
together/ listening to each other/ listening

to this haunting presence/refusing to play dead/
                                        stay dead/

stand on any corner of the fire city, look west to death

after Eve Ewing

we come from fire city, it's been so for generations.
we show the whites of our teeth, to put you at ease.
we real cool*, sound & safe. down in the ashes of our homes,
we know how to conceal, the flick of flames,
through practice. we advise you to not come any closer,
not to touch our hair, say, or our anointed skin. we know.
we burn our own lips before we speak of our tiredness
& frustrations, before we call out your actions for what
they really are. don't look at the sun, yes that hot.
we lie down, spread out ruby, vermillion, red lapping waves,
building an alternative world when fire kissed truths burn
our birth into freedom & laughter & love.

*homage to Gwendolyn Brookes too x.

Resurrection

She came early June the third time she was born,
in 1942, with caster oil and gun power.

She says on losing the sight in her right eye
not to worry none as her third can see just fine,

could see that crowd of men crawling through
the grassland coming to touch her and her kind,

long before the first screams were heard throughout
the village. So why didn't she raise the alarm?

The second time she was born was down south
amongst the new city smog.

The only beauty to be found was between the cracks
and reflected within the black water, her face.

But she's known blood and bones, tooth and claw. Red.
But still her heart beats to a tune of joy.

She's wanting to taste the whole rainbow
through her tombstone-toothed grin.

Now resting in the meadow, she's pressing seeds
into the dark moist earth trusting in their bloom

because for her fourth coming, she'll swell with secrets.
Know how to float the whole universe within her womb.

A true seal doesn't need to be told her worth, she wears the crown

'We are Queens and we do not need you to crown us.'
Jessica L Hagan

Like grey seals entangled in nets, thrashing,
we hurt ourselves, bend into unnatural
contortions to help you to acknowledge us.

From being in close contact with you, we carry the cuts
   & scars.
We squeeze our bodies back into tight caves,
make ourselves non-threatening for you. You. You. You.

In distress, our breathing constricts, we cough
& wheeze, reveal the shape of our ribs & spines.
Blood from our mouths prove we are alive. We hope. We try.

Like a true seal on a beach at rest,   moulting,
these traditions are passed on for safety. For fitting in.
Yet
                            I

                                                      resist.
I thrum with desire,
       floating
           in on
            a tide juicy with self-love.

Away   from   your gaze, I bask in my own light.

Body large, flesh   spreading
             over
          smooth rocks,

slapping my belly, sending   out the alarm.

Can you hear it?

As a true seal
on land or sea (as I'm agile & graceful, everywhere)

I'm unapologetically barking out my J
                                    O
                                     Y

LAYER IV

akin to a child-like wonder

long legs glide through tall grass & wood chippings
it's too early for blueleg brownies, for their smooth heads
but still she looks for them on cool summer evenings, with
moon dropping from a lilacblue sky, air cracking with promise, &
wound gaping where she allowed a lover to settle & then leave.

she looks for the young chestnut brown caps, wavy & sticky
to the touch, relying on her herbwives' blood from ancestors,
remembering them burnt at the stake taking their mushroom
wisdom with them.
            she looks to the magic within the land for healing,
for noticing the beauty of the things around her again.

long slender stems sliding through tall grass & wood chip, in a blue
autumn, will bruise blue, like popping dark blue veins,
                                      when touched
                                      when damaged.

dark morels nestle under my left breast, wide & soft

dark morels
cluster against the roots
of ash trees, moist
in the gathering dark
night air, leaning
into a well-earned
textured silence,
through an arena of trees

night's skin
seeping cold
under a circling mist,
the water knows all.

i rise into a quiet
softness, melting
words onto the page
conjured from embers
& howling dogs

what do I know
about vibrating
at a higher frequency?

yolk yellow lichen
scatter over boulders
like blossom/ verdant hope
nestling under
a humming black sky

i know nothing
of the darkling sky
as compass or map
but i stuff my heart
with moss & fruitkeys,
blood & root
to grow closer to myself,
closer to this land
& the stream of life.

Morchella Elata – Black Morels

Fruits from March to June in corpses, woodland & mulch.
To survive under such harsh conditions, is deemed
   a strength.
Sometimes resilience & resistance can be tiring & dangerous.

Fewer seen in the north of England & from Scotland,
an egg-shaped cap & hollow creamy stem.
A sea of grinning white faces torment the standing body.
You do not belong here.

With the honeycomb appearance, flesh varies from pale
brown to grey & dark to black with age.
Got the scent & the rope to bind the body. To take. To kill.

The work of the devil, poisonous when raw, good when
fried in butter & served on toast.
Into the night air, filled with their laughter,
flames dance naked, sky high.

women within the earth will welcome me once more

from my window,
silent memories shuffle
upon the sea's velvet skin
a darkling chill creeps as I wait
for the women within the earth
to roll closer, stretch out
their slender red arms
to claim my wailing womb

'When a woman pushes a person out of her pussy it transforms her'

after Krista Franklin

into a death machine world
programmed to churn out weary scar scripts
& daylight suffering, we, Black girls
are mothers who are forced
to birth ourselves

/wounded/

it's our skin tattooed with fear
& the desire for magic that
betrays us

with the slitting of the veil,
the most fertile midnight
descends to absolve dis-ease
offering new ways of being

/breathe/

& recognise
within our wombs exist a cosmos
within our bodies a river of bliss & pleasure
sourced from ancestral & mythical struggle

i kinda wanna crack horology wide open

a black quiet line
fades into the archives

to dance is to live

we've been crippled
through time & space

& my eyes & heart

are just opening to the truth
of it all now

or was it tomorrow?

water keeps us flowing/fluid & connected
water has a perfect memory

will lead right back to the source

Africa. the motherland. the mother.
my mother, her womb, my first home,

can I get back?

you flatten out time & space
to steal, exploit, beat & kill
like everything else you've done
to the Blackbody.

we created an empire for you
to abuse with conjured time
& you still acting like a
master c(l)ock.

LAYER V

Llyn Manod, Gwynedd

We climb in the rising heat, and I feel heavy.
Rucksack clinging around my waist like a troll,
I'm at the end of the line, always, as if I need
the others, fitter and whiter than me, to pull me
up the steep pass. I tell myself, I'm taking my
time to savour the moment, enjoy the views as
my breath escapes like a monoprint; white lake
surrounded by shades of grey: flint, slate, gun-
metal to charcoal. The majestic mountain.
Because I'm afraid to love, I keep my wetsuit
on and enter on foal legs the clearest blue lake
known locally as bottomless as well as home
to a water dragon. The dragon does not scare
me. However, letting go does.

Praise to the Lupine

'Beauty can be considered another name for love.'
Anonymous

She is purpley-blue in colour.
When you come close,
you gain her scent.
She will cling to your clothes,
cling to your skin,
invading your senses,
invading your Earth.
Some judge her as alien,
as someone or something
who doesn't belong.
She ignores them and blooms
on her own terms.
In her gorgeousness,
there is light and joy and love.

Listen

... to the geese gathering
honking at all hours, they have arrived
to wait out the winter on these shores

Listen

... as they take to the clear sky
together, in formation, whining, clucking,
as their wide wings caress the cool air

Listen

... in times past, you have missed
this display, missed their joy, because you
were lost to yourself. Not this year.

Listen. Look. Love.

Learning to Breathe with/in Nature

I learn their names the way I learn
to breathe under whiteness with practice.

Beech trees, bare branches
with golden oval leaves rustling at roots.

Bright orange berries, bunching in bulky bushes.
Hardy firethorns bob with blazing bluster.

Like the backs of my hands, rough-lined trunks
sliced by blooming, rubber toadstools, bracket fungi.

To be on the inside, is naming the parts necessary?
Is something, say, a country only brought into existence
once it is named?

Who are you bird who sings now, fledged upon the air?
Your voice echoes our bodies' connection.

The first crisp days of autumn give them to me

'I found God in myself and I loved her fiercely.'
Ntosake Shange

In the silent browning of the air, bedeck my flesh with leaves.

I am Black & from the Earth.

Taste this loss of hunger as the weeping light washes me clean like rain.

Rain, 'tis the season of rain. But with my ever-expanding body, I welcome
the fevered river from the sky.

These violet wings used to fly.

My soul is sirened by brown.

Druridge Bay, Northumberland, 2021

after Hana Meron

i remember the sea's surface. turbulent.
like me locked in fear trying to write poetry. again.
the sky throws shade towards the water. i took
to walking, the story goes, walking out my terror,
the sand damp & clinging, placed me in my body
brought me face to face with my struggle. Baldwin said
you think your pain & your heartbreak
are unprecedented but then you read,
but he hadn't met me by the water's edge,
liminal space disappearing. trying to be love.
the rotting seal pup's body, drew the crowd
not wanting to look away. i walked on
unprotected. i breathed like the north sea,
for a moment, deep & wide & free.

we only protect what we love

after Michael Soule

your brain sends a message to the adrenal gland
from here adrenaline, dopamine & norepinephrine
are released into your body
– the rush & quick of a beat
– the rush & push of a flush

passion. real. & raw.

the lion is circling your camp, the instinct to protect
crouches in your gut ready to pounce & destroy

whales & elephants & blk women
m e g a f a u n a
d e c r e a s e
a whole heap of species is dying
whales & elephants & blk women

As a child I wandered lonely, aimlessly along the streets
of Bradford. Leaves on & off the trees. Cherry blossom
on & off the trees. Rain & drizzle. Sun & wind. Being
at home in nature. Being at home in self. A hunger
for dangerous creatures lured me away, deep
into the belly of the system.

the earth cradles the bones of our ancestors
& we are haunted by state-sanctioned blk deaths
filling our screens while you sit in privileged denial

cyclones & hurricanes
droughts & rising seas
forest fires & factory farming fishing

beigecaramelcinnamonmochamolassesblackertheberryblue-blk
blk heaven blk earth blk universe blk whole

what have whales ever done to you?

i am becoming my mother

'If Black women were free, it would mean that everyone else would have to be free, since our freedom necessitates the destruction of all systems of oppression.'
The Combahee River Collective

Dehumanising the Blackwoman. Mammy, Jezebel, Sapphire, Bitch. The Blackwoman is seen as one dimensional; the mule of the world, carrying the heavy burden of mothering all others except her own. Her own children are lost; lost to the auction block, the ocean, the noose. A Blackwoman is a source of strength and love. Passing on power as well as pain. Her body carries stories, carries histories, carries archives.

as a Blackwoman,
resting deep within the meadow,
held in softness,
grass tickling shins,
dress billowing about
like blossom,
is a political act.

LAYER VI

Playing Palimpsest

1. [water]

'All water has a perfect memory and is forever trying to get back to where it was'.
Tony Morrison

because during the Middle Passage enslaved Africans jumped overboard to freedom
because during the Middle Passage sailors threw cargo over board to lighten the load
my ancestors sprouted gills to fly

                          through
                          water

& birthed a whole nation

hearing their calls
on the waves
i'm drawn to
the waters
that rush
with ease
upon the shore

2. [discourse]

JJ Virey, the author of the study of race standard in the early 19th century, contributed a major essay to the *Dictionnaire des Sciences Médicales* (1815), which settles the polygenetic argument through the acceptable medical discourse concerning the sexual nature of Blackwomen. He writes that Blackwomen, their 'voluptuousness' is developed 'to a degree of lascivity unknown in our climate, for their sexual organs are much more developed than those of whites'.

3. [home]

because my dad died we made our home in
newcastle upon-tyne
because all the time i was living he was dying
because he was diagnosed with leukaemia
when i was 3 months old with only 6 months to live he lived for a
further 9 years
he lived so long because of the love of a
good woman he said a good Blackwoman

(*aside*: I only knew about my dad's illness after his death. Mum
and him agreed to not tell us, my sister and I, about any of it. They
must have thought they were protecting us.
I have had issues with trust ever since.)

4. [white woman]

within my family there are white women
white women who married Black men

1915   my great grandfather sails
from the Gold Coast

a stoker on a merchant ship
to dock in North Shields

i imagine the evening's
bruised purple as boats
bob in port like seals

in theatres   under candlelight
sailors sip rum
to ease tense muscles   & watch

great-nana rosa a wee ginger lassie
dance with seven veils
she enjoys the effect her swinging hips
& pointed toe   has on them

but   night   is   still night
this man with the darkling skin
is pleasing & kind

telling her tales of far-off places
she can never reach

she plans to keep him close   turning her back
on the tongues of the morning sky

5. [white man]

A widely read essay by Sander L. Gilman titled, 'Black Bodies, White Bodies: Toward an Iconography of Female Sexuality in Late Nineteenth-Century Art, Medicine, and Literature' is cited as revealing the hidden nature of Blackwomen. Gilman a white man, therefore his 'facts' and 'theories' are accepted.

6. [a black woman reduced to her sexual parts]

[the sexual parts, the gentialia, the buttocks are the Blackwoman]

(*aside*: If she'd been in a zoo she'd have copulated with the apes because of her deviant sexual appetite that could never ever be sated. Do it anywhere, anytime, with anyone because she can bring out the savageness in any brute. So, it was/is believed.)

7. [history]

when archie rowe asked me out in middle school, he wanted us to keep our courtship a secret. we met behind the garages, through the school yard. he kissed me & played with my tits. [did i just use the word tits? there i've done it again] tits. i was well developed for me age. full blown blossomed boobies. boys will be boys. behind the garages, sprigs of pussy willow wept. shhh it's his secret. too ashamed to be seen with a Blackgirlwoman.

8. [exhibit]

Because in 1810, in London, there was a public scandal as Saartjie Baartman, tricked from the veld of South Africa, was exhibited naked with her 'protruding' buttocks exposed to be poked and pulled, pinched and squeezed like an animal, in a cage, in a zoo.

When the Victorians saw the Black female, they saw her in terms of her buttocks, and saw represented by her buttocks all the anomalies of her sexuality. In a mid-century caricature of the Hottentot Venus, a white male observer views her through a telescope, unable to see anything but her buttocks. Becoming known as the Hottentot Venus, Saartjie died within 5 years of coming to England, at the age of 25.

In death, they could finally have a look under her apron. Cut her body up, pull her body apart. All bodily parts exposed and dissected like an insect, a specimen, a flower. Skin waxed, brain pickled, genitals fossilized and put on display in a museum. To be observed as natural history.

9. [shame]

there's a weight on your chest, on your back
tufts of meadow grass, plantain, yarrow

tufts of meadow grass, plantain, yarrow
creeping bent that reaches to the sun

creeping & bent, you reach for the sun
showing what you look like matters now

what matters is showing who you really are
no matter what they think or say about you

what you think & share should be what's important
but shame's blanket thickens around past wounds

shame thickens like a blanket around past wounds
it's a weight on your chest, on your back

10. [conjure]

These are my two Nanas. Mother and Daughter. Great Nana Rosa on the left is mother to Nana Amber on the right. One white with ginger hair, the other Black with cinnamon freckles. I knew them both as Nana. One birthed my mother, the other brought her up. I come from a long line of women. Women who know trauma. We all know trauma. It's alive in all those who have survived. They say first second, and third generations have the scars. I know my Great Nana Rosa was disowned by her family when she married a Black man. I know my Nana Amber, lost her teeth when she tried to bleach them white along with her skin. Both knew how to keep house, bake and tell stories. Both were resourceful and eager to please. I wish they'd left me more clues, more messages from which to conjure their lives from. I wish I'd listened harder. As a family, as a people, we have an archive of silence. We have many blanks in our histories. I create now to fill in the gaps behind me and in front of me. I bring to life what is within and without. I do so with words and images. My Great Nana Rosa was honorary Black. She suffered because of the choices she made. I thank her for that as I would not be here otherwise. But she was still white. And always would be. And I will always be Black.

11. [experiment]

James Marion Sims is credited as the 'father of modern gynaecology.' Sims developed pioneering tools and surgical techniques in relation to women's reproductive health.
Being a plantation doctor, he was allowed easy access to enslaved women's bodies. In his writings, Sims described the pain that Lucy, one Blackwoman, endured as he experimented on her body. 'Lucy's agony was extreme… she was much prostrated and I thought she was going to die. That was before the days of anaesthetics, and the poor girl, on her knees, bore the operation with great heroism and bravery'. Sims was of the belief, along with others of his time, that Blackwomen could endure all types of pain because they just didn't feel pain. Therefore no need for anaesthetic or any form of pain relief.

12. [body]

i go to the sea full of doubts & worries & self-hate for this body i live in. i spend 10 minutes in communion with the waves. i squeal like the little girl i was & never could be. & when i exit & look down upon my body, swimsuit clinging to all the lumps & bumps, water dripping off my ruby raw chocolate skin, i feel like the goddess i am. i feel alive. & this only happens through the body. my body. here & now, i'm grateful for this body that i experience the world through. this is why (one reason why) i return to the sea so i can carry these treasured feelings toward myself throughout my day into whatever situation i find myself. holding these feelings of self- love like a lantern in my chest that can be rubbed to release the magic genie of love whenever i need that boost. whenever i meet somebody's hate, i can meet it with love.

13. [ocean]

Ellen Gallagher, an African American artist, in her *Watery Ecstatic* series of drawings and paintings of marine life and scientific imaginings, considers the ways in which 'the Atlantic Ocean wasn't simply a conveyance of the slave trade but was a geography rife with meaning: a place of transformation from human to cargo, a graveyard for people whose place on land had been called into ruthless question.'

14. [trauma]

Trauma can be defined as anything that overwhelms the nervous system. Memory, cognitive function and our ability to imagine are all affected by trauma. The stories we tell are deeply affected by trauma. There are blanks in our stories as details cannot be retained. The details are lost. Dr. Michael Skinner, a professor in the School of Biological Sciences at Washington State University, revealed through epigenetic research within each of our cells are approximately three generations of trauma.

15. [mother]

i ain't sorry. she said sticking her chin out at such an angle so she could fix to the spot with her good eye her mam. her mam with her light beige skin & cinnamon freckles, who still has a full set of pearly white teeth at this point. but who would go on to lose them all as she bleached them again & again. who also passed on the habit of straightening her hair to all her daughters. including the oldest now standing in front of her who chooses to no longer straighten her hair after she woke up one morning and found it all on the pillow. just like the birds singing from the few trees out by the back yard, she ain't sorry that she's leaving home, & all that she knew by choosing to marry the Blackest man she's even met & loved. she ain't sorry that she's taking her wide arse away from the narrow streets to make a home with him in bradford. there, the sky may be greyer & the air thick for choking. but she knows in her body that she'll have a better chance of sweet cherry blossom there in his arms than she would ever do under her mam's warped & unloving roof.

16. [rape]

'Rape, as racially constructed, is something that only happen[s] to white women; what happens to black women is simply life.'

From the times of enslavement, the Blackwoman's body has been taken without consent and used by the white man for gratification and economic wealth. Through forced reproduction and exploitation, the stereotype has been perpetuated that Blackwomen are more sexual experienced with heightened sexuality as a means of justifying the sexual assault and violence against them. Blackwomen are viewed as the least likely to be harmed by sexual assault and violence.
Hence, if a Blackwoman has the courage to cry rape, and seek justice, juries and judges are less likely to believe her. Judged against the standard of 'true womanhood' which is the white woman, Blackwomen are judged as hypersexual, of little worth or value beyond the experimentation of forced sexual acts fostering the belief that Blackwomen are unrapeable.

17. [selkie]

under the moonlight, a seal comes upon the seashore. here she discards her skin to become a woman to dance upon the sand. together with her kin, she dances & makes merry under the caressing moonlight. when the sun rises, it's time to retrieve their skins & return to the underwater world. within this liminal space, the meeting of land & sea, anything is possible. this space, where the veil between the living & the dead is at its thinnest, magic happens & shapeshifting is possible. i believe i'm a selkie in reverse, discarding my skin on land as i take to the waters, become a seal, a sea creature of old. going back to my ancestors living upon the seabed.

18. [human]

Pardon I Human
she says
when they cage her
like an animal
to abuse her

Pardon I Human
she says
when they watch her
parade her wears
& ask her to smile.

Pardon I Human
she knows
when they satisfy
their curiosity
& fear spills out like dis-ease.

Pardon I Human
she knows
when he pokes her
with his cane,
to check if she's real

Pardon I Human
she feels
when they display
their disgust
make her a monstrosity

Pardon I Human
she feels
when they pull back
her apron to jeer
& peer deep inside

Pardon I Human
she believed
when she signed
a contract promising
money & return home

Pardon I Human
she burns
when she longs
to see the veld instead
of ugly (white) faces

Pardon I Human
she senses
when they wax her skin
& fossilize her genitals
& pickle her brain

& put her on display
in a museum
for years to come
she continues to be
a freak show in death

Pardon I Human

19. [beauty]

shrink, in every which way you can, & you will be loved.

(*aside*: Brought up under white supremacy culture, the beauty standards are fed to us through the media, screens, books, barbie dolls, and education. There is only one way of being considered beautiful by others & by ourselves; white, slim, straight good long glossy hair and blue eyes.)

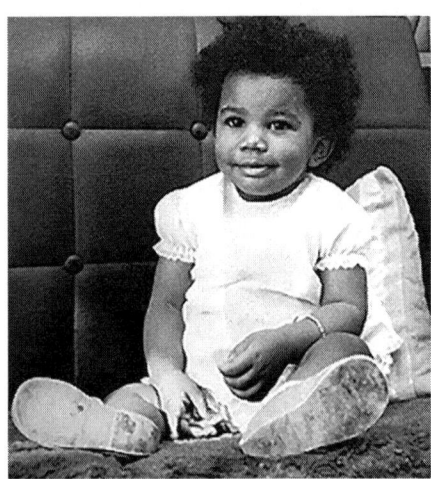

20. [birth]

because i was born white
& my mum rejected me.
because my hair was jet black
& straight & my nose straight too, my mum told the nurse to take

me away, that I was not her baby.
because my Nana rang my dad telling him that he had finally fathered a son in England.
because he had to snub out his cigar & pour out his port
when she rang back to tell him
i was not his son

i was a girl

i am a Blackwoman

LAYER VII

healings

sea salt wound
I smell you
a darkness coming for me

to stop & breathe & be
in the indigo light by the sea

in their soothing caress
waves whisper
        the secrets
        they hold to me
        about me

shimmer light shiver light silk light
water & me

[mother calls me]

womb is the ancestors

shiver moon

      milky light

            marram grass vetch &

mother mountain

       calling me home

             they dwell in us

                darking deep
                like the sea

  the womb is the place
  you'll find me

       moon of the sea, swallowed in me

aftersong

within the touch of
wolves & waves
sea skin belongings
grow within the internal
rhythm of breath
be me
be insolent sea

Surrender into Blackness

inspired by Ayana Zaire Cotton

let me declare doorways,
corners, pursuit, let me say
standing here in eyelashes, in
invisible breasts, in the shrinking lake
in the tiny shops of untrue recollections,
the brittle gnawed life we live,
I am held, and held
Dionne Brand, *Thirsty*

The blackness will swallow you if you allow it.
A darkness so total it promises to disappear you.

You realise this is the bottom. There is nothing beneath, further down,
or coming to save you.

You accept your fate as to fight or to frail will be futile.
With patience & care, you will find comfort in blackness.

Softing open. Making home in the ruins. In the nothing-leftness.
You will come to see the gift of blackness.

Darkling darling, slowly as your eyes become accustomed to the blackness
you will make out other eyes. Pairs of eyes there in the blackness with you.

You are not alone. You are not lost. You are held in the intimacy of the hold.
No voices. No names. No return. Not as you will know it.

But you make do, you make mend of broken bloodline through ritual,
song & dance & love.

You will grow to love the blackness. Grow into blackness.
You will make blackness your home,
       my darkling,
         home.

Notes

Cento for black birds pushing against glass
This Cento is composed of lines from my poems of mine which were themselves partly composed from lines taken from various other creatives. The title is from Lucille Clifton, and other lines are borrowed/acquired/stolen from James Allen, Kara Walker, Tafisha A Edwards, Ocean Vuong, Nicole Sealey, Billie Holiday, Martha Collins, and Toi Derricotte. There's also a nod towards the film *Monster's Ball* (2021) directed by Marc Forster.

The archives will never collect us in a good light
The italicized quotations in sections 2 and 5 are from Rt. Hon. The Lord Scarman, OBE, *The Brixton Disorders, 10–12 April 1981, Report of an Inquiry* (Penguin, London, 1981). The italicized quotation in section 3 is from Luvvie Ajayi, *I'm Judging You: The Do-Better Manual* (New York: Holt, 2016).

go seek help
Renisha McBride, a 19-year-old African American woman was murdered on 2 November 2013. Renisha had been out drinking. On her way home she had a car accident. Disorientated, she got out of her car to seek help. Renisha knocked at the door of Theodore Wafer, a white homeowner. Without talking to her, Wafer fired a shotgun through his screen door and killed Renisha. He claimed it was self-defence. In September 2014, Wafer was found guilty of second-degree murder, manslaughter, and possession of a firearm. He was sentenced to a minimum of 17 years in prison.

How can a mother get over the decomposition of her baby's body in the back of a black cab?
Sarah Reed suffered with mental health issues since the death of her baby in 2003 and was also a victim of police brutality in 2012. Sarah was found dead in her Holloway Prison cell by 'self-

stagflation' on 11 January 2016. While in Maudsley Hospital in 2014, Sarah was sexually assaulted and defended herself. Instead of her attacker being charged, Sarah was charged with GBH with intent. Sarah was sent to prison. Instead of being kept in a psychological facility, where she would have continued to receive the support she needed, Sarah was held in Holloway prison on remand from October 2015 awaiting psychiatric reports before a possible trial. Sarah shouldn't have been in prison.

how many more black women have to die in police custody?
See Kali Nicole Gross, 'How Many More Black Women Have to Die in Police Custody?', *Huff Post* 10 March 2016

Conjur Women
The Combahee River Collective, a Black feminist lesbian socialist organisation formed in 1974, was known for developing an intersectional approach towards the different systems of oppression within society. Calling out racism within the white feminist movement at the same time as the sexism within the USA Civil Rights movement, the Combahee River Collective developed the Combahee River Collective Statement, which clearly stated that because Black women were suffering under all kinds of oppressions. To elevate the Blackwoman's position would mean everyone in society would benefit from the changes. The message in part 3 is from Barby Asante, *Declaration of Independence* (Newcastle upon-Tyne: Baltic Art Gallery Intervention, 2019). The statement in part 5 is from 'Feminist Activism 1968–2018', Symposium (Newcastle upon-Tyne: Northumbria University, 2019)

back-in-the-day-memory as told by a black poet
The phrase 'the sea is history' is from Derek Walcott, 'The Sea is History', in *The Poetry of Derek Walcott 1948-2013* ed. Glyn Maxwell (Farrar, Straus and Giroux: New York, 2014).

Don't sacrifice your skin for anybody
Title from a poem by Emmy Fisher.
For information and inspiration see
www.iceland24blog.com/iceland-and-viking-settlement
and
http://issuu.com/rvkgrapevine/docs/issue02_2017_lowres

how can we climb through the hold of the ship once more to come out moved?
I would use 'transmigration here to mean movement across and also the movement from one form to another', Christina Sharp. See *In The Wake*. Also Saidiya Hartman, 'A Venus in Two Acts', *Small Axe*, Number 26 (Volume 12, Number 2), June 2008.

found poem: we arrived here with stars in our hair and needles between our toes
See Paul Taylor, 'Black Aesthetics', *Philosophy Compass* 5 January 2010 and drea brown, 'Conjuring the Ghost: A Call and Response to Haints.' *Hypatia*, vol. 36, no. 3, 2021.

'When a woman pushes a person out of her pussy it transforms her'
See Maria Eliza Osunbimpe Hamilton Abegunde, 'The Blackest Most Fertile Midnight', in Franklin, Krista. *Too Much Midnight*. (Chicago: Haymarket Books, 2020).

Playing Palimpsest
Section 2: see Julien-Joseph, Virey, 'Femme' in *Dictionnaire des sciences médicales* (Paris: Panckoucke, 1815).
Section 5: see Sander L Gilman, 'Black Bodies, White Bodies: Toward an Iconography of Female Sexuality in Late Nineteenth-Century Art, Medicine, and Literature' in *Race, Writing and Difference* ed. Henry Gates Jr. (Chicago and London: University of Chicago Press,1985).
Section 8: see Rachel Holmes, *The Hottentot Venus*. (Bloomsbury: Random House, 2006), Sadiah Qureshi, *Peoples on Parade: Exhibitions, Empire and Anthropology in Nineteenth Century*

Britain (Chicago: University of Chicago Press, 2011), Janell, Hobson, *Venus in the Dark: Blackness and Beauty in Popular Culture* (London: Routledge, 2005).

Section 9: this verse-form is a duplex – a combination of the sonnet, the ghazal, and the blues – invented by the poet Jericho Brown.

Section 11: see J Marion Sims, *The Story of My Life: J Marion Sims* (Cleveland, USA: D Appleton and Company, 1888).

Section 13: see Carolina A Miranda, 'Painter Ellen Gallagher's tragic sea tales: How African slaves went from human to cargo on the Atlantic', by in *Los Angeles Times*, 17 November 2017.

Section 14: see Michael Skinner, 'Ancestral ghosts in your genome', TEDxRainier, 5 January 2017.

Section 16: see Lisa Crooms, *Symposium: Speaking Truth to Power: The Jurisprudence of Julia Cooper Mack: Speaking Partial Truths and Preserving Power: Deconstructing White Supremacy, Patriarchy, and the Rape Corroboration Rule in the Interest of Black Liberation* (1997)

Section 19: see Chimamanda Ngozi Adichie, *We Should All Be Feminists* (London: Forth Estate, 2014).

Surrender into Blackness
'What is terrifying partakes of the abyss, three times linked to the unknown. First, the time you fell into the belly of the boat. For, in your poetic vision, a boat has no belly; a boat does not swallow up, a boat does not devour; a boat is steered by open skies. Yet, the belly of this boat dissolves you, precipitates you into a nonworld from which you cry out. This boat is a womb, a womb abyss. It generates the clamor of your protests; it also produces all coming unanimity. Although you are alone in this suffering, you share in the unknown with others whom you have yet to know. This boat is your womb, a matrix, and yet it expels you. This boat: pregnant with as many dead as living under the sentence of death.' – Édouard Glissant, *Poetics of Relation.* cited in Christina Sharpe, *In The Wake: On Blackness and Being* (Durham and London: Duke University Press, 2016).

Acknowledgements

Grateful acknowledgements are made to the editors of the publications in which versions of these poems and essays within this collection first appeared.

'[white women]' a collage poem here first appeared in *Family Album*, Flambard Press, 2011 and *A Properties of Silk*, ID on Tyne Press, 2013. 'Don't sacrifice your skin for anybody', *Something Other*, 2017; 'Listen', *Nine Muse Poetry*, 2019. 'healings', 'womb is the ancestors' and 'aftersong', are taken from the self-published zine, *wolves and waves*, 2022. 'i am becoming my mother' is part of a creative essay, 'I Am Becoming My Mother: Conjuring Black Motherhood On Our Own Terms' in *The Mother Wave: Theorizing, Enacting, and Representing Matricentric Feminism* edited by Andrea O'Reilly and Fiona Joy Green. Demeter Press, 2024. 'Cento for black birds pushing against glass', '[frog-march]', 'how can we climb through the hold of the ship once more to come out moved?', 'stand on any corner of the fire city look west to death', 'A true seal doesn't need to be told her worth, she wears her crown', 'akin to a child-like wonder', 'we arrived here with stars in our hair and needles between our toes', 'we only protect what we love', and 'i am becoming my mother' were published in a chapbook published by The Wildheart Press, 2024.

The writing of this book was enabled by grants from the Society of Authors and Arts Council England.

Works Cited

Romare Bearden, *Conjur Women*, The Studio Museum in Harlem, 1964
Gwendolyn Brooks, *The Bean Eaters*, Harpers, 1960
Jericho Brown, *The Tradition*, Picador, 2019
Ayana Zaire Cotton, *Seeda School Newsletter,* 2024
Robin DiAngelo, *White Fragility: Why It's So Hard for White People to Talk About Racism*, Beacon Books, 2018
Eve Ewing, *1919,* Haymarket Books, 2019
Franz Fanon, *Wretched of the Earth,* 1961, Penguin 2001
Krista Franklin, *Too Much Midnight,* Haymarket Books, 2020
Jessica L Hagan, *Queens of Sheba*, Nouveau Riche and Soho Theatre, 2015
Sharon Hall Hurley, *Sharon's Anti-Racism Newsletter*, 2024
Hana Meron, *Kaleidoscope Black Newsletter,* 2024
Ntozake Shange, *for colored girls who have considered suicide/when the rainbow is enuf*, Simon & Schuster, 2010
Leath Tonion 'We Only Protect What We Love – Michael Soule on the Vanishing Wilderness,' *Sun Magazine,* 2018
Thompson, Mary Reynolds. *Reclaiming the Wild Soul: How Earth's Landscapes Restore Us to Wholeness*, White Cloud Press, 2014